USBORNE FIRST READING

Level Three

USBORNE FIRST READING

The Three Little Pigs

retold by
Susanna Davidson
Illustrated by Georgien Overwater

Retold by Mairi Mackinnon
Illustrated by Frank Endersby

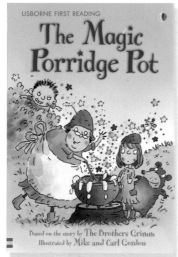

USBORNE FIRST READING

The Magic Porridge Pot

Based on the story by The Brothers Grimm
Illustrated by Mike and Carl Gordon

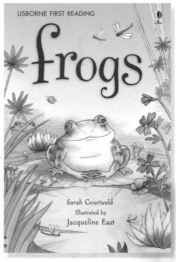

USBORNE FIRST READING

frogs

Sarah Courtauld
Illustrated by
Jacqueline East

D0335037

The Owl
and the
Pussycat

Edward Lear
Illustrated by Victoria Ball

Reading Consultant: Alison Kelly
Roehampton University

The Owl and the
Pussycat went to sea

in a beautiful
pea-green boat.

They took some honey

and plenty
of money,

£5

wrapped up in a
five pound note.

The Owl looked up to
the stars above and sang
to a small guitar.

Oh lovely Pussy!
Oh Pussy my love...

What a beautiful
Pussy you are, you are,

what a beautiful
Pussy you are.

Pussy said to the Owl,

you elegant fowl,

how charmingly sweet
you sing.

16

17

Oh let us be married —
too long we have tarried.

But what shall we do
for a ring?

They sailed away...

...for a year and a day,

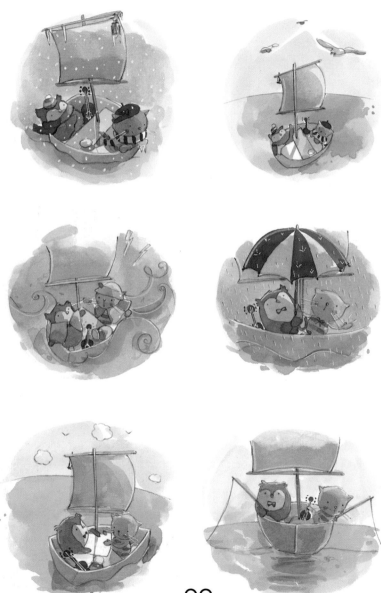

23

to the land where the
Bong-tree grows.

And there in the wood

a Piggy-wig stood,

with a ring at the end
of his nose,

his nose,

with a ring at the end
of his nose.

Dear Pig, are you willing,

to sell for one shilling,

your ring?

33

Said the Piggy,

I will!

So they took it away,

and were married
next day,

by the turkey who lives
on the hill.

They dined on mince, and
slices of quince,

which they ate with a
runcible spoon.

And hand in hand,

on the edge of the sand,

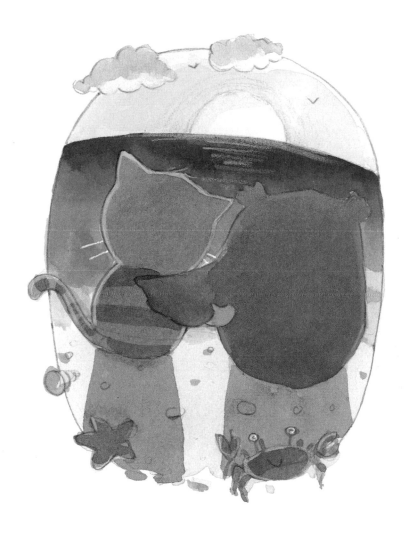

they danced by the
light of the moon,

the moon,

they danced by the light
of the moon.

About Edward Lear

Edward Lear was a Victorian poet
who wrote lots of poems for children.
He lived with his cat Foss and he also
loved painting birds and animals.

Illustration by
Edward Lear

Designed by Michelle Lawrence
Edited by Sarah Courtauld
Series designer: Russell Punter
Series editor: Lesley Sims

First published in 2008 by Usborne Publishing Ltd., Usborne House,
83-85 Saffron Hill, London EC1N 8RT, England. www.usborne.com
Copyright © 2008 Usborne Publishing Ltd.

48

USBORNE FIRST READING
Level Four

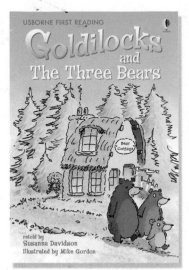

Usborne First Reading
Goldilocks and The Three Bears
retold by Susanna Davidson
Illustrated by Mike Gordon

Usborne First Reading
The Emperor and the Nightingale
based on the story by Hans Christian Andersen
Illustrated by Graham Philpot

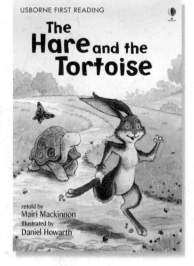

Usborne First Reading
The Hare and the Tortoise
retold by Mairi Mackinnon
Illustrated by Daniel Howarth

Usborne First Reading
Butterflies
Kate Davies
Illustrated by Jana Costa